A Pony fo

By Iris G

D0563482

Easy Reader Book

This book is an *Easy Reader* book for children just beginning to read on their own. They may need help with a few words, but will enjoy the independence of reading the story about ponies.

(Possible readers ages 6 to 8; can be read aloud to younger children. See notes on page 33 for additional helps.)

Iris Gray Dowling
Philippians 4:13

Faithful Life Publishers
North Fort Myers, FL 33903
FaithfulLifePublishers.com

Copyright © 2012 Iris Gray Dowling

ISBN: 978-1-937129-50-7

Published and printed by:
Faithful Life Publishers
3335 Galaxy Way
North Fort Myers, FL   33903

888.720.0950

www.FaithfulLifePublishers.com
info@FLPublishers.com

Illustration work by Valerie Bouthyette.

Printed in the United States of America.

18 17 16 15 14 13 12   1 2 3 4 5

Table of Contents

"I'd like a pony for my birthday" said Garth.

Chapter 1

Garth's Birthday Wish

Eight-year old Garth waited at the neighbor's house until Mom came home from work. As soon as he saw her, he ran to her and started talking. "My birthday's coming soon. I know you didn't forget, did you, Mom?"

"Of course not," she replied. "How could I forget that you'll be a year older and wiser."

"Mom, I'd like a pony for my birthday," he said.

"Honey, since your Dad had to leave for active duty, we don't have money to buy a pony. We don't have enough money for our own food. The pony has to have a place to stay and it costs a lot to board and feed one at the farm. You can have a birthday party, but we can't afford a pony," she said as they went in the house.

"Mom, I don't mean a pony to keep—just one to ride for my party. That's all the guys talk about at school," said Garth as he sat down at the table.

"I don't know how we can do that either. We'll have to play, 'Pin the Tail on the Pony'.

"No-o-o-o...Mom! We play that game every year. I want a real pony this time. Remember I told you all the fun we had riding ponies at Randy's party. We rode and rode, up and down his driveway all during his party."

"I don't think I can pay for a pony right now, Garth...Maybe next year. We'll have to do something that doesn't cost so much," said Mom as she put the plates on the table.

Garth laid his head on the table and tried to hide some tears. He thought and thought what to do. Then an idea popped into his head. He wiped his tears on his sleeve and asked, "Hey, Mom, how about if I earn some money to pay for the pony?"

"I don't think you can earn enough in one month. You won't have too much daylight to work when the time changes next week," said Mom.

"Please, let me try, Mom? I'll start by helping you right now," he pleaded.

Garth got the clothes out of the dryer, folded them, and put them in the right drawers. Garth felt sure he could earn enough money to get the pony.

Every night Garth did the chores Mom had on her list. On Saturdays he raked leaves for his grandparents and neighbors. In the next few weeks he did lots of jobs, but still the money wasn't enough. *What can I do? I don't have enough time to earn money*, he thought.

As he scrubbed the kitchen floor for mom, he remembered the money his Grandma gave him last summer. She said to save it for something special and Mom made sure he did.

Garth thought, *What's more special than having a pony for my party?*

When Mom got home from work he asked her in a shy tone of voice, "Mom, couldn't I use the money Grandma gave me? She said to use it for something special. The pony is something special for me. That would make enough so I could get a pony."

Garth's eyes got brighter as he waited for Mom's answer, "I guess it won't hurt, but you really need some shoes for gym," she said with a little smile.

"Mom, I'll get the phone. Could you call Mr. Roy to see if he can bring the pony December seventh? Here's the number." Garth handed her a ragged piece of paper he had gotten from his friend, Randy.

Mom pushed the numbers: 215-520-1406. Garth watched as she asked Mr. Roy to come. Without a word she smiled and laid the phone down. Garth waited for her reaction.

Why is she so quiet, he thought as he edged closer to her. Finally he couldn't wait any longer so he asked, "Mom, can the pony man come?"

"Oh…yes, Garth. He said he'll come at two o'clock on December seventh, only if the weather is good…It sometimes snows in December, you know."

Garth went on doing his chores to earn money for the pony. After dinner he ran the sweeper in the living room. "Mom, is there anything else I can do tonight?" he asked.

Mom saw how serious Garth had been about earning the money. She said, "Maybe you should go to bed early tonight. Tomorrow is Saturday and you have a yard job to do. Grandma also wants you to wash her car and help put up her flag for Pearl Harbor Day."

"Okay, Mom, I like doing that. She puts the flag up every year for my birthday," he said as he went off to his room.

After a good sleep Garth got up early and ate breakfast. He was about ready to leave for his first job when Mom asked, "Have you thought who you're going to invite?"

"Yeah, the boys in my class. We'll dress like cowboys and Indians. That's what we did for Randy's party."

"You'll need to think about getting some invitations ready," said Mom.

"Randy's going to help me make them on his computer. May I go to his house today when I get my jobs done?"

"That'll be all right, Garth. Call me when you're done making your cards and I'll pick you up."

Garth worked hard all day to finish his jobs. In the evening he and Randy created some neat invitations.

On the front they placed a picture of a cowboy riding his pony. They put horseshoes in a circle around the cowboy. On the inside pages were small colored pictures of cowboy hats, guns, boots, and ropes. The message read: *Please come to Garth's Pony Riding 'Birthday Party on December 7 at one-thirty. Wear your cowboy or Indian clothes.*

When Mom arrived Garth carried his cards to the car. He smiled and said, "My next job is to pass out these cards in my school class on Monday."

"You seem a year older already," Mom joked.

"That weatherman has to be wrong. I hope he made a BIG mistake!"

Chapter 2

Disappointments

As the party day got closer Garth couldn't get the birthday party out of his mind. At school he daydreamed. He thought about the pony 24/7. He didn't think much about his lessons, though. Waiting for the party day seemed worse than waiting for Christmas morning.

The December days got colder and every day Garth rushed home from school to hear Al, the TV weatherman. *Just four days before my party*, he thought. His eyes and ears opened wide when he heard, "A band of snow is coming from the southwest. Snow will start around midnight."

Oh, no! It can't snow! What can I do? he thought.

That night a few snow flurries darted past the window. As Garth got ready for bed, he said his prayers before Mom came in to say, good-night. He prayed, "Dear Lord, please make the snow stop! Amen!"

After Mom tucked him in, he laid awake listening to the wind whirling around his house...*Whoooo-ooh-ooh.* It rattled the windows,...bang...Bang...BANG!

He wondered why they didn't break. Sometimes the whistling wind sounded like music, but not to Garth's ears. A few times he jumped up and stared out into the dark night. *That weatherman has got to be wrong*, he thought. *I hope he made a BIG Mistake!*

With his face pressed on the window he saw a few flakes swirling and whirling outside. *They were **Real!** and **White!** and **NO Mistake!*** he thought.

Soon he crawled back in bed and his eyes drifted into sleep.

The next morning the ground had a coat of white. Snow flurries scurried everywhere. *At least it's not so bad. School is not closed,* he thought. He put on his boots and went: crunch… Crunch… CRUNCH…to the school bus.

Later as he sat in class thinking about the pony, a message came over the intercom: School is closing at noon. Not until then did he look out the window to see how much snow had come down.

By the time he stepped off the school bus near his house the roads had gotten slippery. He saw the snow piling up in his driveway. Each time he thought about the pony he felt a little sick at his stomach. *There's no safe place for a pony to walk*, he sighed.

Mom came home from work early, too. All afternoon she saw Garth's sad eyes stare out the windows. Any other day he would have been out playing in the snow.

"Stop! Stop! STOP!" he shouted as if the snow could hear.

"Maybe you could make a snowman with ears," joked Mom.

"Oh, Mom, he couldn't do anything to help this problem."

"You could change your plans to have a sledding birthday party," she suggested. "You could also have a contest to see who can make the biggest, best snowman."

"That's NOT funny, Mom! STOP JOKING! I don't want a sledding party!" he grunted.

"Don't you think a pony can pull a sleigh?" she asked.

She realized Garth wasn't in a joking mood, so she said, "I'm sorry, Garth. You can still have a party. Would you like me to bake you some pony cookies that taste like gingerbread?"

"Okay. Thanks, Mom." Still he wondered if he'd be able to have a REAL pony.

The snow came down all night. Garth thought, *how will all this snow melt? I do know God can send lots of sunshine and warmer weather if he wants to.* That night before he got in bed he folded his hands and asked God for more help.

As Garth lay in his bed he thought, *tomorrow I need to shovel the snow out of the driveway so the pony can walk safely.* He shoveled himself into dream land.

The next morning he put his hands over his eyes to keep the bright sunlight from blinding him. He rolled out of the bed and shuffled over to the window. Sunlight made the snow glisten like sparkling diamonds, but it didn't look pretty to Garth. He wanted it gone…Gone… GONE…even if it did mean he'd have to go to school. *Since I don't have school, I had better get to work*, he thought.

He got the shovel and lifted his feet up and down in the deep snow. *There is a lot of snow out here. I wish Dad could be here to help me,* he thought.

About noon when Garth came in to rest, he found Mom in the kitchen mixing cookie batter. He plunked into a big chair and clicked on the TV news. Al, the weather guy, said, "Snow plows are working hard to clear the main roads. It will take another day to plow the country roads. Just stay in your homes and enjoy some hot chocolate. The temperature may rise tomorrow and the warming sun will melt some of the snow. Then the kids will be able to go back to school."

Beaming from ear to ear Garth leaped up, out of the chair and ran to find Mom. She was in the dining room trimming a fake tree with colored lights and sparkling balls. "Yippee! Al says, 'it's gonna get warm. The snow's gonna melt.' The pony can come tomorrow. That's awesome, isn't it Mom?"

"Yes, Garth. See your Birthday Tree. I thought I'd dangle the cookies from its branches. Do you see some are shaped like ponies, some like boots, and some like cowboy hats. For Pearl Harbor Day and your birthday I put little flags around the base of the tree—one for each boy to take home," she said.

"Cool, Mom! It's different from any Birthday tree I've ever seen. I really like it," smiled Garth as he started back to listen to more of the weather report.

"Garth, didn't I hear the weatherman say the country roads weren't plowed yet? You know Mr. Roy's farm is on a country road," added Mom.

"I think the snow's gonna melt tomorrow morning. I'm going back out to push more snow out of our driveway so it will melt when the sun comes out."

"I'll be ready for your party," replied Mom, but she doubted if all that snow on the roads would be gone in time.

On Garth's birthday morning the bright sun beamed in his window and in his eyes, so that he could not sleep. The sun seemed to say, *Get up, you sleepy head! Birthday boys can't stay in bed!* Garth popped up and put on his cowboy clothes. His shirt was brown and red with dangling black frills. He had a holster, but no guns. Mom didn't allow him to play with guns.

He tromped down stairs and found Mom fixing the table. "Do you think the pony will come?" he asked.

"Let's wait for an hour or so to call Mr. Roy and make sure he's coming," Mom said.

That hour seemed longer than all day. Garth paced up stairs and down stairs. He stared at the piles of snow near the street corners. His toys waited. So did his favorite books. He only worried and dreamed about whether the pony could come. Finally, he watched Mom put the rest of the light blue icing on his favorite chocolate cake. In the middle she put a cowboy wearing a red shirt with black frills—just like his.

The musical clock on the wall chimed each half hour. The time between half hours seemed so-o-o-o long. Finally Garth heard, BONG!...Bong!...Bong!... ten times for ten o'clock. Then the phone rang.

Garth quickly ran and grabbed the phone. Handing it to Mom, he anxiously waited to hear the news. He could hear Mr. Roy's faint southern voice saying, "I can't get the trailer out of the snow today. The roads out near my farm are not very good for hauling ponies. It's not safe to ride them even if I could get to your house." Garth gulped and tried not to cry. His throat swelled a little when he thought of how hard he had worked for this day and now he couldn't have the pony.

Chapter 3

There Is Hope!

Garth heard Mr. Roy's voice speaking again. "I know Garth really wanted the pony so much. Since I can't come today, if you can have the party tomorrow afternoon, I'll let him have two ponies for the same price. I think some snow will melt and I'll be able to get my trailer out by then. Or you can bring the boys to my farm. They can ride around on the two ponies in my inside corral. I'll even hitch up the sleigh and Cinderella can take them for a jingle bell sleigh ride over the hills."

"Give me a few minutes to talk this over with Garth, and I'll call you back," said Mom.

Garth looked sad when Mom suggested that the sleigh ride sounded like fun. "No, Mom, I want the ponies to come to my house. I can go to the farm some other time."

"Okay, Garth. It's your party. It'll be a lot easier to have the party here. If we go to the farm we won't have enough time for all the other fun and food I've planned," agreed Mom.

She called Mr. Roy to tell him Garth wanted the ponies to come to his house the next day at the same time. After that she started making more phone calls to Garth's friends about the change.

The next morning Mom got the table ready with blue plates, red candles, white forks, and cowboy napkins. She added bowls of potato chips, vegetable chips, and popcorn. Next she put the cookie tray in the center of the table. Around one o'clock she put the juice and ice on the table. "Your friends will be here soon. "Garth, can you think of anything else I need?" she asked.

"It's okay, Mom."

Garth heard the clock chime at one o'clock: **B**i**ng…Bong!** He anxiously waited for the next **Bing**… that meant...***One-thirty!*** His serious look turned into a smile when he heard: ***Tap…Tap…TAP!***

"Neat-O!" said Garth as he threw the door wide open. Four boys in cowboy outfits with western holster belts tromped in:. ***Tromp...Tromp…Tromp****!* Behind them tiptoed three more in tan frilly Indian clothes carrying their bows and arrows. *"**Whoop-opp-pee**"* they yelled. Each one put a present on the smaller gift table.

Mom brought in the decorated cake with nine flickering red, white, and blue candles. The boys sang: *"**Happy Birthday, Garth!**"* He blew out all the candles with one big puff. Mom served the cake, cookies, popcorn, and punch to the noisy, hungry bunch.

When they got done eating each boy decorated a big bag with all kinds of stickers: cowboys, guns, holsters, boots, hats, Indians, feathers, drums, ponies, cows, calves, flags, and more.

"I have big red, white, and blue balloons and flags for each of you. I'll put them with your bags," said Mom.

"Why can't we have balloons now?" asked Shawn.

"Mr. Roy told me to hold all balloons until the end. It isn't good to have balloons near the ponies when children are riding. The pops could scare the ponies and make them jump.

"Jumping is fun!" said Shawn.

"The kind of jumps I'm talking about wouldn't be safe for all of you," said Mom.

The clock struck two...*Bing! Bong-ong-ong!*

"Mom, where are the ponies? Mr. Roy said he'd be here at two."

"I'm sure he's driving slower because of some snow on the country roads where he lives."

"Here, open my present, Garth," said his friend, Jimmy.

Garth ripped the paper off. "a bow and arrows. Wow! Just what I want when I play Indian. Thanks, Jimbo!"

Now open this one from me," said Randy handing it to Garth.

"I know what's in it. A rope! Thanks, Randy," said Garth as he threw it around the chair. Randy grabbed the rope and started to spin it. With that, Garth ran to the window. "Mom, the ponies aren't here yet."

"They'll be here soon. Why don't you see what's in this letter from your Grandma?" Mom said as she handed it to Garth.

He opened the card and read:

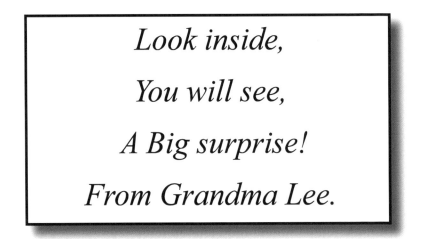

Look inside,

You will see,

A Big surprise!

From Grandma Lee.

He looked under the folded part of the card and found some money. Another note read: *Use this for your trip to the farm next spring.*

"Thanks, Grandma, but I'm not going to the farm", he said as he dashed over and pulled the curtains back to stare out the window. At that moment he saw the truck coming. "Wow! It's for real! The ponies just got here!"

Seven excited boys squeezed through the doorway. Each boy tried to be the first one out. "Wait! Wait!" Mom called, "Wait on the steps until Mr. Roy gets the ponies ready."

"Hi-i, ya-all," said Mr. Roy in his southern voice as he led the ponies out of the trailer. "I'll put the saddles on before you can say, '*Ride 'em, cowbo-ey'.*"

The boys repeated those words because they liked the sound of Mr. Roy's southern voice.

He put a shiny leather saddle on the little white pony with gray specks all over her face. Her tail and mane were as white as the snow. "This is Cinderella," said Mr. Roy. Doesn't she look like she rolled in the cinders, just like in the 'Cinderella' story?"

"Yeah, ya-all," the boys answered as they pranced around trying to see who could stay first in line. They repeated Mr. Roy's words again and again: "*Hi-i, ya-all; Ride 'em, cowbo-ey.*"

Mr. Roy put a brownish western saddle on Camelot, the bigger grayish pony with a thick blonde mane and long, blonde tail—reaching down to the ground. "This is Camelot, named after the rich prince," he said as he pulled the girths tight. "I have to tighten these girths so you and the saddle won't slide off the pony and land on the ground. Now-ow, I think we're ready."

The boys pushed to be first in line. Garth edged close to Mr. Roy and said shyly, "I'm really happy you came."

"Are you the birthday boy?"

"Yep, that's me!" Garth answered proudly.

"Hey fellows, can we let the 'Birthday Boy' ride first?" Then we'll let ya-all ride."

No one seemed to mind since that's what Mr. Roy did at their parties, too. "Garth, what pony do you want to ride first?

"I like Camelot because he is bigger and moves a little faster and bumpier," said Garth. He grabbed the saddle horn and pulled himself up in the saddle, like a proud cowboy.

"Here, hold the reins with this hand and the lasso rope in that one," Mr. Roy said.

"I remember what you told me at Randy's party. Neat-O! Giddy-up," Garth kicked Camelot's sides as he smiled at Mom. "Aren't you going to take my picture?" he asked.

Grandma aimed the video camera right at Garth. He and Camelot trotted up and down the driveway in front of her. When he smiled his eyes looked like sparklers on the Fourth of July.

Mr. Roy helped the next rider climb on Cinderella. Dressed in his Indian suit, Jimmy and Cinderella trotted behind Camelot. Her gait was a little slower and smoother, but Jimmy said, "I like her gait best. She walks like a princess."

"I like Camelot, he's faster," said Shawn.

"I like Camelot, too. He walks like a prince," said Randy.

All the cowboys and Indians took turns riding up and down the driveway until an hour had passed. Mr. Roy snapped polaroid pictures—one of each boy as they sat on their favorite pony.

Finally, Mr. Roy announced, "Camelot and Cinderella have worked hard to make you happy. Now let's make them happy. They want to go back to the farm and rest until the next party."

Chapter 4

Going Home

"I wish they didn't have to go," said Garth.

"They know when the party time is over," said Mr. Roy.

"Do they wear watches?" joked Garth.

"No, they have built in clocks. They have gone to so many parties they seem to know exactly when the hour is up. Watch while they get in the trailer. They jump in much faster than they get out because they know it's time to go home."

"Oh-h-h. Let me see how they go back in the trailer," said Garth.

"First, let me take the saddles off; then you can lead them in," said Mr. Roy.

After he took the saddles off, he handed Garth each lead rope and motioned for him to walk in the trailer ahead of the ponies. They went in so fast that Garth had to run to get out of their way.

"Wow! Look at them jump in!" said Shawn.

"They look just like big puppy dogs," said Jimmy.

Garth looked so surprised that Mom and Mr. Roy started laughing. All the boys laughed, too.

"I think the ponies DO know it's time to go home," said Garth.

"Ya-all got that right," said Mr. Roy as he fastened them in the trailer. They also like their birthday cake.

"Birthday cake? What birthday cake?" said the boys.

"A big pile of fresh hay," said Mr. Roy as he pulled some greenish hay up for them to see.

While Mom went in the house to get the bags and balloons Mr. Roy gave each boy his picture of the pony ride. The parents smiled as they looked at the pictures of their sons riding their favorite pony.

Mom gave the bags and balloons to Garth so he could give them to all his friends. "Now that the ponies are in the trailer, you can play with the balloons," she said.

"Thanks, guys. Thanks for the presents. Thanks for coming to ride the ponies with me. See ya-all at school on Monday." The boys waved good-bye to Mr. Roy, then they waved good-bye to Garth.

Everything suddenly got quiet. Garth turned to Mr. Roy and gave the old farmer a big hug, "Thanks for bringing Cinderella and Camelot to help celebrate my birthday party," he said.

Mr. Roy hugged Garth. "I'll see you next spring when the weather is a lot nicer." Garth's eyes seemed to have question marks instead of pupils in them. "Remember Grandma's card?" said Mr. Roy. "She planned another surprise for you. You're coming to my farm."

"Wow! That's so-o-o cool!" Garth said as he hugged Mr. Roy once again. Quickly he ran and threw his arms around Grandma Lee. He was so busy thinking about the ponies coming to today's party that he didn't realize what she had given him. "Thank you, Grandma. Thanks for letting me ride the ponies again. You're the greatest Grandma a guy could have!"

"Do you think you can wait until spring?" asked Mr. Roy.

"I'll get to see Cinderella and Camelot, won't I?" Garth asked.

"Of course, you will. You can brush them and comb their manes and tails. Then you'll ride them in the big corral for as long as your mother will let you stay. They will be all yours for the afternoon," said Mr. Roy.

"Yippee-yi-yay! I'll be a real cowboy once again!"

"That's right!" said Mr. Roy as he shook Garth's hand. He put the trailer's tailgate up and fastened it carefully, then got in his truck and started the engine.

"Thanks, Mr. Roy. Thanks for bringing Cinderella and Camelot. You made me have the happiest birthday party ever."

Garth waved good-bye to Mr. Roy and the ponies. "Good-bye Camelot, Good-bye Cinderella," he called as they rode away.

"I'll see you next spring," said Mr. Roy as he drove away leaving Garth to his world of dreams.

"What an awesome party! Thanks, Mom. Thanks, Grandma." Then Garth folded his hands and looked up. "Thank you, God for sending the sunshine and the ponies. Thank you for the greatest Mom and Grandma in the whole world!"

Book Dedication

Dedicated to Cle, Rob, John, Joe, Fred,
and all those who helped make pony rides
an enjoyable event in the lives of children.

Pictures on the opposite page:

Top: Camelot

Middle: Cinderella

Bottom: Children enjoying pony rides
at a pony party.

Notes to the Parents
of Beginning Readers

- This Easy Reader Book is written to help keep the young reader's interest high.

- It is told in simple, interesting style with a strong rhythm to add enjoyment both for reading aloud and silently.

- The parent can read the story first to encourage the child to listen and then the child can read on his/her own.

- This Easy Reader Book will help most children realize they can have fun reading on their own.

- Most First and Second graders will read this story independently, but if needed a little help should be given for encouragement.

- This book shows how the young reader can have a successful experience in problem solving.

- This book shows how friends help and care about each other.

- This book teaches respect and good manners.

- This book promotes understanding for military families when a parent has to serve away from home.

- This book helps the young child realize God cares about him/her.

CPSIA information can be obtained
at www.ICGtesting.com
Printed in the USA
LVIW011029230912
299764LV00001BA